The Adventures of Jack Stone-Hard
Written by Jack Stone & Jessica Cunnilingus

The Adventures of Jack Stone-Hard

First edition. May 10, 2021

All images are taken from Pixabay.com.

Attributions (Pixabay tag), in order of appearance, below:
Disappointed woman (Snap_it)
Girls Gossipping (Cuncon)
Man with knife (Sammy_Williams)
Worried woman (rickfanwilsen)
Preganant woman (marcelobragapublicitario)
Spaceship (Papafox)
Captured woman (Engin_Akyurt)
Amazon Woman (darksouls1)
Cardinal (WikiImage)
Man with Flowers (Free-Photos)
Tavern sign (suju-foto)
Templar (Janson_G)
Fit man (deepkhicher)
Spaceship outside castle (Inactive_account_ID_249)
disappointed man (Schäferle)
Disappearing woman (ShiftGraphiX)
Pirate (sik-life)
Sexy redhead (JerzyGorecki)
BDSM girl (4557712)
Knives (rihaij)
Space soldier (TheDigitalArtist)
Dead woman (Victoria_Borodinova)
Woman in nature (Binja69)
Shirtless man (Deedee86)
Naked woman (528928)
Wormhole (Genty)
BDSM Girl (Victoria_Borodinova)
Asian girl (allphotobangkok)
Supernova (eli007)
Planet and star (eli007)
Alien woman (fantasticpicture)
Fitness couple (FamilyPhotoStudio)
Female robot (KELLEPICS)
Woman in warehouse (Victoria_Borodinova)
Amazon woman (monsieur_raddar)

I0734744

Jack Stone-Hard and the Orion Pendicular Tryst.

"Ahh!"

Megan Hart moaned in disappointment as her husband Tom finished another lovemaking session both too early and too late. Too early as he came before her, too late as he could have kept going until tomorrow and he still wouldn't have hit the G-spot. He was that bad.

"Was it good for you too?" Tom asked, as it would seem, oblivious of his shortcomings as a lover.

"Uh-um, yes my love." Megan replied, even though her inner voice screamed: 'You're doing it wrong, Goddammit!'

Megan forced a smile towards Tom. She would remain peaceful for now as there was no point in fighting after her husband had ejaculated. If she wanted to rile him up, she should do so before the fucking took place, to bring out his inner beast. Megan had doubts whether there was such a thing in the weak Tom, but she hoped to one day release it, so she could have enjoyable sex for once.

As Tom fell asleep, Megan reflected on things. How had life come to this? Megan realised that she had herself to blame. Due to her fervent religious beliefs in her youth, she had opted to be a virgin when she got married. When she turned 18, her raging sexuality had been impossible to contain. To deal with it, she had done the only thing she could do to reconcile God's will with her sexual needs. She had gotten married to her first suitor. Not trying before buying had been a stupid idea, and she had suffered a decade of unfulfilling sex as a punishment.

Her sex life had started disappointing, and it had gone downhill as time progressed.

Megan studied herself in the mirror. She had used to be gorgeous and intelligent in her teens, but she wouldn't rate herself as attractive anymore. Being stuck in a dead-end relationship with a loser, snacking in front of the TV appealed more to her than the treadmill. As a result, an unsightly amount of lard covered her body. While she wasn't obese yet, she was far from the hottie that she once was, and she wondered if anyone else in the world would be interested in bedding her.

Megan pouted her lips towards the mirror and smiled. Her mouth was still great for sucking cock, and Megan imagined the salty flavour of a large bratwurst deep down in her throat. Delicious, yet it was just a dream.

"If you are not happy with Tom, you can always come with me to the brothel. There is a good selection of handsome men there." Megan recalled her friend Jessica's words. She had brushed them off as silly at the time. However, now was the time to act on Jessica's advice. Megan needed a good fuck; she needed a beautiful man to fuck her as he meant it.

'Hey, Jess. Keen to take me to the brothel on Orion Pendicular tomorrow?' Megan texted, turned off her phone, and fell asleep.

***

Jack Stone-Hard was gathering the blood-covered gold teeth of the assassin he had fought against. He recognised the man he had fought in low gravity on his small smuggler's vessel. He had fought Josef Goldteeth from the Castro Cartel, which was the largest criminal gang in the Orion star system. The assassin had got him with a few strikes before he turned the fight around when he knocked the teeth out of his assailant with a haymaker punch. After knocking out the gold teeth of his assailant, Jack had finished Josef off by shoving him into the airlock and ejecting him to the freezing space.

Jack grimaced as he studied his reflection. Josef had stabbed him in his

torso with a serrated knife, and the pain made him cringe. He needed to seek medical attention before he left the Orion star system. Although he didn't think that the stab wound had severed any of his organs, he would rather not find out the opposite, once he was in interstellar space.

"Uh-um, yes my love." Megan replied, even though her inner voice screamed: 'You're doing it wrong, Goddammit!'

Jack pulled off his shirt and studied his torso in the mirror. He was a towering man, made of raw muscle. He stroked his hand over the stabbing wound. He hoped that Josef hadn't laced the blade in poison. However, if he had, it was game over, and there was only one more thing to do. He needed to get one last good fuck before he clocked off!

Jack doused whiskey on his wound, bit down on a wooden fork, and stapled his wounds with a stapler to stop the bleeding. It wasn't pretty, but if he survived this, he would have a sexy scar as a memory.

After sealing his wounds, Jack set the course for Orion Pendicular. The trading post had everything he needed before he left the Orion system. There was a discreet doctor that wouldn't ask any questions and a brothel where he could unleash his raging masculinity.

***

"Are you not having a good time, Megan?"

Megan looked at her friend Jessica, who seemed excited to be at the largest brothel on the Orion Pendicular. The brothel was a smorgasbord of everything a woman could desire in men. There were black, white, yellow, blue, and green men in all forms and shapes, yet they all lacked what Megan wanted the most. Megan wanted a man who had a raging desire for her, she wasn't keen to fuck someone who saw her as his next pay check. She was already the breadwinner in her marriage, and she didn't desire another loser who depended on her, one way or the other.

"No, I don't think I came to the right place," Megan replied.

"Why is that? Are you having second thoughts about cheating on Tom?" Jessica asked.

Megan shook her head and replied. "No. I

want to fuck someone who desires me."

"Honey. We are in a brothel. These men are jacked up on pills. They will get hard and

fuck you for a long time." Jessica replied.

"Oh, I don't know," Megan replied.

"Alright. Suit yourself. I'll fuck this one tonight." Jessica replied, approached a tiny Asian man with a golden face mask, and grabbed his crotch.

"That one? He isn't even well-hung." Megan objected.

"You got to try them all. I have already tried the green man with three nipples, the black man with the huge plutonium cock, and the white hawk-eyed guy with the steel abs. Each has given me different sets of experiences. This will be another one to my collection." Jessica said and led the Asian man to a private room.

Megan sighed. She wished that she were as sexually liberated as Jessica, but she wasn't, and she had not found what she was looking for in the brothel. 'I guess I'll head home and have some disappointing sex with Tom again,' Megan thought to herself, finished drinking her Cosmopolitan, and left the brothel.

***

"Hey, you. Where are you going?" Megan froze as a few slimy members of the Castro Cartel armed with knives and tasers waylaid her as she left the brothel via the backdoor.
"I am going home," Megan replied.
"Sneaking out via the backdoor? Are you running away from your bill? We will make you pay for fucking us over, bitch." The Cartel member threatened.
"I am not running from my bill. I didn't fuck anyone in there." Megan mumbled and stared in terror at the Latino gang with black lenses.
"Are you dissing the brothel of the Castro Cartel? Now you are dead, bitch!" The man hissed.

"Leave her alone."

Megan looked at the man who had spoken. An air of raw masculine sexuality surrounded him, and she felt how her pussy was soaking. This was an effect that none of the man-whores at the brothel had on her.
"Oh, look who is here. Jack Stone-Hard.

How dare you enter our territory?" The cartel member said.

Jack took out a zip-lock bag with gold teeth from his pocket, chucked them at the man's feet, and spoke. "Josef Goldteeth is dead. This gold should cover my debt, Sebastian."

Sebastian stared at the gold teeth in awe, looked at his men, and spoke. "You'll die for this insult, Jack!"

Having said this, Sebastian and two other cartel members fired their tasers at Jack. Jack clenched his jaw, flexed his muscles, and resisted the electric shock. Two cartel members stormed towards Jack with drawn knives. Jack dodged the first attacker and pulled the arm of the second attacker to stab the first attacker. After that, he headbutted the second attacker and finished him off with a knee to the nuts.

Seeing this, the other cartel members ran away.

"Hurry up and come with me!" Jack exclaimed. Megan nodded and together they ran to Jack's smuggler's vessel to leave the trading post.

***

Ten minutes later, Megan and Jack were on Jack's ship, on their way to Orion Prime.

"Leave her alone."
Megan looked at the man who had spoken. An air of raw masculine sexuality surrounded him, and she felt how her pussy was soaking.

"So, what were you doing in that alley?" Jack teased.

"Uhm, I-I-I….." Megan stuttered shyly, her cheeks flushed like roses.

Jack laughed and replied. "Hahaha. Don't worry. We all have needs. But don't make a runner on the Castro Cartel unless you can fight."

"I didn't make a runner. I didn't fuck anyone in there." Megan replied in indignation.

Jack smirked and pulled off his shirt to see if he had any wounds from the fight.

Megan stared in awe at Jack's beautifully shaped torso. It was full of tattoos, scars, and sexy hard muscles. One of the wounds looked fresh from the stitches. Her pussy was wetter than ever, yearning for his cock.

"Oh my God. You are injured." Megan exclaimed.

"I will be okay," Jack replied.

"Umm, is there anything I can do to make you forget about your pains?" Megan asked.

Jack nodded and licked his lips.

Megan took the hint, approached Jack, got down on her knees, and unzipped his pants. She grabbed his cock that was getting harder by the second. She tasted it. It was the perfect bratwurst and to her great relief, it was clean. She started sucking Jack's beautiful cock and it amazed her how big it became. She had never had anything this big in her mouth before, and it was a challenge for her cock-sucking technique to avoid using her teeth.

'Challenge accepted.' Megan thought and she moaned excitedly as it reached its maximum size. She tried swallowing the whole behe-moth in a go, but she couldn't, and her eyes became watery as she gagged.

Jack pushed Megan's head backwards, turned her around, and had her leaning over a table. He pulled down her panties and rubbed her clitoris with his manly but gentle hands until she climaxed and squirted all over the floor.

Jack entered her and fucked her furiously from behind. Getting fucked like this, Megan's mind transcended time and space. She knew one thing during the exhilarating experience. She wanted to have Jack's baby. A man like Jack was worthy of spreading his genes, and he would give her what Tom couldn't, a strong child.

As Jack came, Megan collapsed to the floor in exhaustion from the multiple orgasms she had experienced. When she had recovered, Jack was back in the driver seat of the space-craft.

Megan approached him and kissed his neck.
Jack spoke. "I am taking you back to Orion Prime. I need to leave this star system. The Castro Cartel will keep hunting me."

Megan looked at Jack with a mix of sorrow and desire. A part of her wanted to come with him. His cock was an addictive drug that she already yearned for again. As if he could read her mind, Jack said:

the life I am lead-
your normal life
this night for what it
"Thank you for
like a woman again,"

"Getting fucked like this, Megan's mind transcended time and space. She knew one thing during the exhilarating experience. She wanted to have Jack's baby."

"You don't want
ing. Go back to
and remember
was."
making me feel
Megan said.

Jack nodded, dropped Megan off near her home at Orion Prime, and left without saying a word.

As Megan came home, she jumped her husband and rode him possessed. Jack had fucked her well and ignited her inner her long-gone lust ignited, even her doofus husband enough to make her hit the right spot!

as if she were
lust. With
was

***

Megan looked at the positive pregnancy test and smiled. She hoped that Jack was the father, but she wouldn't endeavour to find out. She closed her eyes and remembered her wild night of passion. This memory got her gears going, so she approached Tom, smiled, and said "I have a surprise for you, darling." Having said this, Megan pulled down Tom's pants and sucked his cock sweetly.

Jack Stone-Hard and the Amazon Rescue.

Melanie Bosom shivered as a drop of icy water landed on her bare, well-formed breast. She wasn't dressed for being locked up in this damp and cold dungeon. While she liked showing off her ample forms and great body, she would have preferred a thick jacket on this occasion. 'Fuck it. There are no bad clothes, just bad weather!' Melanie thought. She dreamt of returning to the beautiful beaches of her homeworld on Tau Ceti Secundus, the second planet of the Tau Ceti system which was a tropical paradise in the polar regions of the planet.

Melanie belonged to an Amazon tribe on her planet and there were two things she loved to an equal degree. A good fight and a great fuck. She recalled the best fuck she had ever had. Two decades earlier, Jack Stone-Hard had landed near her village and he had given the many women who lived there the hard cock they yearned for. Any other man would have succumbed to the challenge of satisfying the ravenous hunger of Melanie and her Amazon sisters, but Jack had stood firm. He had fucked them all into exhaustion, going at it for three days straight. Many new boys and girls had been the outcome of Jack's endeavours, but the boys had been sent away to another village. On Tau Ceti Secundus, men and women lived separately, and only met for one purpose. To copulate!

One day, the free sexuality lifestyle of Melanie's tribe had stirred the ire of the Order of the Starry Cross. Religious zealots had landed, kidnapped Melanie, and had taken her away to Tau Ceti Tetra, the fourth icy world of the Tau Ceti system. The zealots had forced her to repent and marry their ugly leader, Grand Cleric Brogdan Dalamir. This marriage had lasted for three days until Melanie had enough of Brogdan's impotence and had fucked his handsome son, Paris, instead. The zealots had locked her up in this dungeon and she had not left ever since.

Thinking of Paris, Melanie got horny, and she started playing with her breasts and clitoris. When she played with her breasts, she forgot about the cold in the damp cell, and soon she was in the blissful realm of frantic masturbation. As she came and squirted on the dirty bed in her cell, she was brought back to reality. Melanie sighed. She dreamt of returning to her tropical homeworld, where she could roam around naked with her sisters and involve herself in orgies with neighbouring male villagers. That was the life to lead.

***

Jack Stone-Hard looked at the fuel tanks in his spaceship. He had enough tri-sentium tanks for four more lightspeed trips across the Milky Way Galaxy. By the time he ran out of tank rods, he would need to find the woman who could satisfy him and keep him faithful. At least he needed to find a planet where his raging masculinity didn't put him at odds with the rest of the population. Jack studied the star map. He was close to his destination, Tau Ceti Secundus. The planet had been the home of Melanie Bosom, who had the best pussy in the galaxy. She was the closest Jack had ever been to experiencing love. He would arrive at Tau Ceti Secundus in a day's travel, which was the equivalent of a month in local time. Such was the effect of time dilation when travelling at lightspeed. Every day Jack travelled, a month went past outside. Thus, even though it felt like he visited the Tau Ceti Amazonians a year ago, 20 years had passed in their time.

Jack thought of Melanie Bosom. When they last fucked, she had been tireless, and he had to push himself to the limit to keep up with her and her Amazonian sisters. Would she still be as amazing now, after all that time?

Thinking back on his tryst with Melanie, Jack had to fight hard to contain his desire to pull down his pants and masturbate. He had been alone on this spaceship for 40 days since he left the Orion System, and he had not ejaculated since. Jack didn't believe in masturbation. It was selfish to waste his raging hormones on himself when there was a whole galaxy of women to satisfy. Besides, he wanted to save everything he had before meeting with Melanie again.

Jack thought of Melanie Bosom. When they last fucked, she had been tireless, and he had to push himself to the limit to keep up with her and her Amazonian sisters.

'One more day,' Jack mumbled, closed his eyes, and meditated to speed up time before the great release would come.

***

Jack felt a sense of familiarity as he landed in the Amazonian village the following day. The next generation of women was as beautiful as ever, yet he didn't feel any innate attraction to them. What was wrong with him?

He walked to the centre square of the village and smiled as he saw the statue of himself with a giant phallic. He was big, but not that big, and besides, the 15-inch pole on the statue would have been too massive to give most women a pleasurable fuck.

The Amazonian Serena approached Jack. When Jack saw her, he had a nice flashback of her wet cunt, yet she was not his prime destination for this visit. Melanie Bosom was to receive his first load, as she was the highlight of his last visit.

"Welcome back, Jack Stone-hard, our Phallic God. It has been 20 years since you last visited us. It is such a great pleasure to witness your return." Serena said seductively.

"Likewise. Where is Melanie? I would like to visit her." Jack replied.

Serena's smile disappeared as Jack mentioned Melanie Bosom. This was tacit recognition of something she had feared for all these years. Melanie was better at sex than she was. Serena brushed it off. It was a silly thing to be jealous about, as Jack and some other travellers had given Serena boundless pleasure throughout the years in the Amazon. She should focus on her satisfaction, not if Melanie was even better than her at fucking.

"Melanie is not here. The Order of the Starry Cross took her away." Serena revealed.

"When did this happen?" Jack said and grounded his teeth.

"Last year," Serena replied.

'Last year. Could Melanie have lasted a whole year of sexual dissatisfaction with those zealots?' Jack thought. Jack felt like he was about to have a temper outburst. As much as he wanted to save his first load for Melanie, he couldn't handle another day of not coming.

"I need to release my frustration." Jack growled like an injured lion.

Serena studied Jack for a moment, nodded seductively, and said, "Please come with me." Jack nodded and Serena led him to her hut. As they got in, she crawled to him

like a tigress, cut off his belt with a machete, shoved him to the bed and got on top of him. 'She is so hungry for sex. She must

have been angry that I asked for Melanie instead. She will surely give me a time of my life,' Jack reflected while smiling to himself wickedly.

As Jack got hard, Serena rode him furiously with her wet and very slimy pussy. 'Mmmmm, she must have been doing lots of kegel practices, she's feels so tight and delicious,' Jack reflected as Serena's wet and delicate pussy gripped around Jack's hard penis tightly, like a perfectly fitting suction cap.

Jack struggled to contain his ejaculation, and he couldn't resist it as it felt so freaking good. Serena wasn't Melanie, so he didn't care enough to push himself to hold it in. He blew his massive load inside Serena's wet and tight pussy, and it overflowed all over the bed.

***

"I need to go. I need to save Melanie from the Order of the Starry Cross."

Serena looked at Jack with a hint of disappointment. He had used her sweet and eager pussy to blow his first load and now he was heading off to save his true love, Melanie Bosom. As disappointed as she was that Jack wouldn't stay longer to satisfy her raging needs, she was also surprised. She had never pictured Jack as a man with strong emotions, and she hadn't foreseen that he would try to save Melanie from the zealots.

"What is going on, Jack. You have been away for 20 years. Why sacrifice yourself to save Melanie." Serena said.
"It hasn't been 20 years for me," Jack replied and thought back on his mistake.

The time dilation that occurred when one took part in Interstellar travel at near lightspeed was a factor that had ruined Jack's life. Jack had been ready to settle down with Melanie when he had a vision that his brother was in danger in the Orion star system, ten light-years away. He hadn't thought twice about coming to his brother's side. However, there was a catch. The Orion system was ten light-years away from Tau Ceti, so when Jack had arrived after travelling at near lightspeed, his brother was long dead. While Jack had dealt with Josef Goldteeth and those that were responsible for his brother's death, he had wasted 20 years of Melanie's lifespan seeking vengeance.

"What do you mean it hasn't been 20 years for you?" Serena asked.
"Time moves differently when one is travelling at lightspeed. It's hard to explain." Jack replied.
"So, do you still love her after all these years?" Serena asked.
"All I know is that I need to save her," Jack said.
Serena nodded and showed Jack a star map. "Melanie is kept a prisoner at New Bethlehem on Tau Ceti Tetra. Be careful, Jack."
"Don't worry. I will get her back." Jack said with his deep and mysterious voice, left the hut, entered his spaceship, and set the course for Tau Ceti Tetra.

***

"You must be Jack Stone-Hard?" An athletic and good-looking man said to Jack, as Jack was drinking red wine in a shady tavern in New Bethlehem. Jack didn't particularly like wine, but it was the only alcoholic beverage that the Order of the Starry Cross allowed on the planet.

Jack gave the young man a cold gaze and

> **"What do you mean it hasn't been 20 years for you?" Serena asked.**
> **"Time moves differently when one is travelling at lightspeed. It's hard to explain." Jack replied.**

replied: "Who is asking?"

"I am Paris Dalamir. I am the son of Grand Cleric Brogdan Dalamir." Paris replied.

"You should have brought more men." Jack sneered.

"You misunderstood me, Jack. I am not here to attack you. In fact, we want the same thing." Paris replied.

"And what is that?" Jack asked.

"We both want to save Melanie. Melanie is a prisoner of my father, and she is his legal wife. The order doesn't allow divorce. We must kill my father." Paris revealed.

"Ha-ha. Why don't you kill him yourself?" Jack mocked.

"Our culture frowns upon patricide. The only way I can succeed my father is if you kill him. Once I have succeeded him, my first order will be to pardon you for his murder." Paris said.

"Why should I trust you?" Jack said with his deep and dark voice.

"Tsk, tsk, tsk. Mr Stone. We both know why you are here. I am giving you the chance to save Melanie. Please accept it." Paris replied.

"What do you need?" Jack asked impatiently.

"This is my key card. Use this card to access my father's private quarters and kill him. The key code is 6969. To deflect suspicions against me, you'll need to knock me out as you leave this tavern." Paris said and handed Jack an electronic key.

Jack nodded and replied. "One more thing. What will happen to Melanie?"

"Melanie will be a widow, and she'll be free to choose her path. I am not like my father." Paris said.

"That is acceptable," Jack said and knocked Paris out with a sucker punch to the head, and then took the key.

***

Grand Cleric Brogdan Dalamir was sodomising a young male priest when Jack entered his private quarters that same night. Brogdan stared at him in surprise and exclaimed with his high-pitched voice, "Who are you, how did you get in, and why are you here?"

"I am here to save Melanie," Jack replied and pulled out a pistol. He shot Brogdan with six shots, one to the head and five to the chest. He turned to the young priest and spoke. "Tell the others what happened here. Tell them that I surrender."

The young priest nodded, grabbed his clothes, and hurried to leave the room.

'Here goes nothing,' Jack thought as he chucked his pistol to the floor and waited for the guards to arrive. He was playing the odds. Trusting Paris's words was a better option than a futile attempt at shooting up the palace while looking for Melanie. 'Love makes us do crazy things,' Jack thought and smiled as the zealots rushed in, beat him into a pulp, and dragged him to the dungeon.

***

Jack was feeling sexually frustrated as he was sitting in the dungeon of the Order of the Starry Cross's stronghold. He didn't particularly worry about dying, as we all got to go some time. However, he was frustrated that he hadn't taken part in an orgy when he visited the Amazon village.

Then he recalled why he had come back to this star system. He had come to feel the absolute pleasure of Melanie Bosom's wet cunt, and no one else was close to that vaginal supremacy in the village.

"Jack Stone-Hard. Come with us, heathen." A guard said.
"Is it time?" Jack asked.
"Yes!" The guard replied. Jack prepared himself to go down in a blaze of glory. He wouldn't fight the guards here. He would fight them in the town square for what he presumed would be his public execution. How else would the order punish him for killing their Grand Cler-

ic?

Much to Jack's surprise, the guards didn't take him to the town square. Instead, they took him upstairs to the Grand Cleric's private residence. The guards opened the door, shoved Jack into the hall of the residence, and slammed the door behind them.

Jack looked in the direction of the voice. He saw Melanie Bosom and Paris Dalamir, relaxing on a couch, both wearing their birthday suits.

"Welcome, Jack. I am so glad that you came to save me." Jack looked in the direction of the voice. He saw Melanie Bosom and Paris Dalamir, relaxing on a couch, both wearing their birthday suits.

"As you can see, I am a man of my word. If it isn't too much of a hassle to you, I would like to witness your unmatched sexual prowess. That is unless you find Melanie unattractive." Paris proclaimed.

Melanie giggled, and she walked up to Jack and unlocked his chains.

Jack didn't waste any time. He lifted Melanie against the wall and kissed her like a starving man who had finally arrived at a buffet. His penis got harder than ever, and he fucked her roughly against the wall while lifting her with his strong arms.

Watching Jack's furious technique, Paris smiled and drank some red wine. It was a miracle to study such a force of nature in action. He had never seen Melanie so soaking wet, and her

screams so filled with raw animalistic joy.
"Melanie, darling. Please come here and suck my cock." Paris teased. Jack sought eye contact with Melanie, and she nodded. He lifted her over to Paris and started fucking her from behind to free up her mouth for Paris's member.

Jack watched how Paris's dick got bigger as Melanie's greedy mouth sucked it like it was the last lollypop in the candy shop. It wasn't as big as Jack's, but it was still an impressive penis both when it came to size and its perfect bend and symmetry.
"Let's swap," Jack said, pulled out his penis and took a step back. Melanie got seated on Paris's penis, rode it reverse cowgirl, and greedily swallowed Jack's dick.

They were having a great time and kept going at it from all angles until the trio collapsed to the floor, drained of genital fluids, and dehydrated.

Paris poured a glass of water, drank it, and spoke. "You have some very impressive moves, Jack. I guess this is the moment of truth. You cannot have us both, Melanie. Make a choice."

Melanie sighed, looked at Jack, and spoke.
"Jack, you are by far the best sex partner I have ever had. No offence, Paris."
"None taken. I have seen Jack in action. He is very impressive indeed." Paris smirked.
Melanie nodded and continued. "Having said that, sex is not everything in life. You left me, and you were gone for 20 years, Jack. Meanwhile, Paris deposed his father to make me the queen of this planet. This is goodbye, Jack."
"Your spaceship is on my balcony. As much as I enjoyed watching you in action, I hope that our paths will never cross again." Paris said.

Jack held back his impulse to kill Paris. As much as he didn't want to surrender Melanie to anyone, he had agreed to let her make the decision. This was her choice, and if this was the happiness she sought for, who was he to deny it?

Without a word, Jack walked to his spaceship and left, never to return to the Tau Ceti star system again.

"Your spaceship is on my balcony. As much as I enjoyed watching you in action, I hope that our paths will never cross again." Paris said.

Jack Stone-Hard and the Mira System Raiders.

Jack Stone-Hard was staring into the empty void of space as he was travelling at lightspeed, and he felt depressed. Travelling at lightspeed was strange as all the light sources were drawn out. Despite being in interstellar space, light surrounded him when he looked through the windows of his spaceship.

Jack had set his destination to the Mira system, which was 40 lightyears away from the Tau Ceti system. This was by design. Once his ship had reached lightspeed, he could not turn it around until he had reached its destination. 40 years would have passed outside his spaceship when he reached the Mira system. This knowledge was enough to stop him from returning to the Tau Ceti system to see Melanie Bosom again.

Leaving Melanie behind had been the hardest thing Jack had ever done in his life. She had rejected him, despite him giving her the best fuck of her life. Melanie had preferred to be the consort of Paris Dalamir, who took control of Tau Ceti Tetra after Jack murdered his father. Jack had wanted to kill

Paris after their threesome with Melanie, but he had stopped himself. He had given his word to respect Melanie's decision, and he had upheld it. Keeping this promise was the hardest thing he had ever done, as he was not used to female rejection, particularly not from the one who stole his heart.

'Don't cry!' Jack thought and contained his emotions. He felt silly. Despite being all alone in interstellar space, the thought that someone would see his softer side terrified him. Jack closed his eyes, meditated, and pictured the many beautiful women he would fuck once he reached Mira Secundus. He smiled. There were billions of women out there in the vastness of the galaxy. Why should he think about the one that got away?

***

A raider approached Captain Morgan Spacebane when they were raiding the Infirmus

Outpost on the Mira Secundus planet. Morgan ignored the raider and continued drawing patterns on his face with the blood of his fallen enemies. The raider cleared his throat and spoke: "Uhhmm, Captain, we have brought all the women suitable for prostitution onto our ship. What should we do with the other prisoners?"

I'll elevate the volunteer to be my concubine."

Most of the women looked at the floor, but one redhead woman stared at Morgan with a defiant look and spoke, "I volunteer. If you are half the man that my husband was, my pussy is yours, from now until death do us apart."

"Morgan smiled wickedly. He had decided to let the weak men on this outpost live to tell the tale."

Morgan got up from his chair and spoke. "Gather all the remaining prisoners in the main hall of the outpost. I will make an announcement before we leave."

"Aye-aye, Captain." The raider replied and rushed off.

Morgan smiled wickedly. He had decided to let the weak men on this outpost live to tell the tale. While it would be safer and more convenient to kill them all, killing them was too merciful. Morgan wanted the weak enemies he had vanquished to live in shame for the rest of their lives. They had cowered in fear and given up their women without putting up a proper fight. To die was an honour he wouldn't give them.

Morgan got up and walked to the holding area of his pirate ship. They had chained all the women together. Morgan spoke to the group, "I am looking for a volunteer that I can fuck in front of the weak and feeble men of this outpost. If I enjoy the fuck,

Morgan gave the redhead a cold gaze and smiled viciously. He had heard about the wild sexual nature of the Mira Secundus women, but he was yet to experience it. He was happy to find a volunteer for his show of strength. While rape wasn't beyond him, he couldn't humiliate the effeminate men of the outpost by raping someone. Morgan wanted everyone to witness his sexual prowess. Only with a willing woman could the crowds hear the loud moans of pure pleasure when he used his huge member to its best effect.

"Excellent. I cannot wait to fuck you." Morgan said.

"Why not fuck me now? I am your prize, Oh mighty captain Morgan Spacebane." The woman mocked.

The redhead's tone infuriated Morgan, and he felt an intense desire to fuck her hard. He calmed down. If he wasted his efforts now, he would put on a poor performance later for his crew and prisoners.

"Your time will come. What is your name?" Morgan said.

"Elvira Shaw." The woman replied.

Shaw… Morgan recalled murdering some-one called Samuel Shaw earlier during the day. That must have been Elvira's husband. This intercourse would indeed be interesting.

"I will see you shortly, Elvira," Morgan said and left the holding facility.

***

An hour later, Morgan Spacebane stood at a stage in the main hall of the Infirmus Outpost. The male prisoners were chained and were kneeling below him. One of Morgan's men held a chain connected to a collar around Elvira's neck.

Morgan spoke to the gathered prisoners, "Weak men of the Infirmus Outpost! I have decided to spare your puny little lives. You do not deserve an honourable death after your craven failure to fight me. Instead, you shall live in shame without women to warm your beds. I will show you how a real man fucks!"

Having said this, Morgan snorted some powder and let out a roar. He grabbed Elvira's chain and dragged her towards him. 'She is hungry for my cock.' Morgan thought as Elvira tried pulling down his pants. 'Or maybe she wants to go down in a blaze of glory?' Morgan reflected and pushed Elvira's mouth away from his crotch. As much as he wanted her greedy mouth to suck his cock, he didn't want her to bite it off.

Morgan turned Elvira around, pushed her over a table and started eating her pussy. Morgan loved the taste of pussy, and what

he loved even more, was the moans of pleasure that Elvira gave out. This would teach the soon to be eunuch male population

of this outpost how to please a woman. As Elvira squirted in his face, Morgan felt satisfied with his cunnilingus skills. He pulled down his boxer shorts and revealed his huge penis to the gasping crowds. He shoved it into Elvira's soaking pussy and fucked her furiously.

'She is enjoying it too much; I better fuck her in the ass.' Morgan thought. He changed from pussy to anus, which changed Elvira's screams from screams of pleasure to screams of pain. After a few hard strokes, he pulled out his penis and ejaculated a massive load over Elvira's back.

Having finished, Morgan gave the signal to his men to carry out his plan. The raiders approached the prisoners with stun guns and shot them in the crotch to turn them into eunuchs. After the macabre display, Morgan and his men dragged Elvira back onto the pirate spaceship and left the Infirmus Outpost.

***

The following day, Jack arrived at the Infirmus Outpost, eager to find a few women to satisfy his raging needs. Much to his dismay, he couldn't find any woman. An effeminate man with a high-pitched voice approached him.

"Greetings, traveller. You must help us. The terrifying pirate Morgan Spacebane attacked us and kidnapped our women." The effeminate man said.

"That is not my problem. I am just looking for a feed and a good fuck." Jack replied.

"We would be happy to feed you. However, a fuck will be hard to provide as Morgan took all our women, and he turned the men into eunuchs." The man replied in tears.

'How do they know I am not gay,' Jack thought, but he let that thought slide. Instead, he replied, "Then feed me and tell me about your pirate problems."

"Thank you, my good sir. You look like the man we need. I am Michael Softdick, and I am the prefect of this outpost." Michael said sheepishly.

"I am Jack Stone-Hard. I am an adventurer and a problem solver." Jack replied.

"Please come with me and I'll feed you," Michael said gayly and took Jack to the canteen, served him a large meal, and told him about their woes.

***

After a few hard strokes, he pulled out his penis and ejaculated a massive load over Elvira's back.

Elvira Shaw entered Morgan Spacebane's private quarter on the PSS Spacebane vessel. Her bum was hurting from the anal sex. Yet, she couldn't forget the immense pleasure from Morgan's pussy eating and the perfect shape of his huge member when he fucked her wet pussy. Morgan was a force of nature and it was a shame that he used his unsurpassed sexual ability in the name of evil.

Elvira shook it off. Regardless of how good Morgan was at fucking, he still needed to die. He had murdered her husband Samuel, and he had turned the rest of the menfolk into eunuchs. For such a crime, there was only one punishment, death. Elvira hated that Morgan had seen through her and kept her mouth away from his crotch during the display of his sexual prowess. No matter, she would get the chance to kill him now as he had summoned her to his chambers.

'She is coming for me.' Morgan thought and smiled. He knew about the knife that she clumsily hid behind her back. What an amateur! Yet it was more fun to play along until the very last moment. By giving her a chance to kill him, he kept his senses sharp.

Morgan embraced Elvira and began greedily french kissing her. She reciprocated his kisses, and a small streak of hesitation reached his mind. When would she try to stab him? The natural choice would be for her to strike straight away, yet she hadn't taken this option and instead, she kissed him with immense pleasure.

'Now!' Morgan thought, and he got his right arm up to grab her arm at the last moment.

Morgan gazed at Elvira and the knife's edge that was mere centimetres away from his throat. A few second of tense staring ensued, but Morgan was in control. He twisted Elvira's arm and punched her hip with his left hand which caused her to collapse to the floor. As Elvira was down, Morgan finished her off with a kick to the face that broke her nose.

"Impressive. You almost fooled me by not striking straight away. Yet you failed, and I will punish you." Morgan said.
"What are you going to do, Spacebane? Are you going to rape me? Bring it on!" Elvira taunted defiantly.

"Tsk, tsk, tsk. I don't need to rape you to get what I want. Women throughout the entire Mira system is lining up to get a piece of me." Morgan taunted and pressed the emergency button next to his bed.

Shortly after that, two raiders rushed in. Morgan looked at them and spoke. "This woman needs to die. Strip her naked and take her to the dock. We will make her death a spectacle." Morgan said and laughed menacingly.

***

Jack Stone-Hard looked at the weak band of eunuchs that had joined him to fight the pirates. They were useless and vulnerable, which was why they had ended up the way they did. Yet, they still served a purpose for Jack. They would become distractions when he stormed the pirate ship to save the female prisoners. Alone he wouldn't have stood a chance against the 30 pirates on the vessel, but accompanied by the 24 eunuch volunteers, he stood a chance. Besides, the eunuchs would fight without fear of dying. Having lost their women and their balls, they had no reason to fear death anymore. Their fearlessness would save the day for the attackers.

"How are we going to attack the pirates? Their ship is heavily armed, and I can't see many armaments on the ship." Michael Softdick said.
"My ship itself is the weapon. This ship is built for lightspeed travel and has an almost indestructible front part. Their ship is not." Jack revealed.
"So, what are you going to do? Are you going to ram them?" Michael asked.
"Yes, the front of this ship has a battering ram with a built-in airlock. If we hit them with enough speed, they won't see us coming." Jack revealed.
Michael nodded and Jack spoke again, "Get your men to brace and prepare for boarding. We are going in hard soon."
"Yes. May God bless us and help us avenge our fallen." Michael said and ran off to alert his men.
'God doesn't care,' Jack mumbled, lit a cigar, and strapped himself to a chair to withstand the impact to come.

***

"Look at your sister, Anna. That is what happens if you betray me."
Anna looked outside Morgan Spacebane's bedroom window. She gasped in shock. Her sister was hanging dead and naked outside, with her skin deep-frozen from the freezing space.
"You monster! What did you do to her!?" Anna exclaimed.
"She tried to seduce and murder me, so she wasn't welcome on my vessel anymore. Unfortunately, the freezing space didn't do wonders for her survival." Morgan laughed.
"God will punish you for this!" Anna exclaimed.
"He is welcome to try. However, let's focus on something more important. We are going to fuck, and you are going to enjoy it. If you don't come, you don't appreciate my efforts, in which case you are no longer welcome on this vessel. Do I make myself clear?" Morgan threatened.
Anna nodded and sobbed quietly.
Morgan smirked and spoke: "You are fortunate that I am amazing at fucking. Get naked and get down on all fours and you might still get out of this predicament alive."

Anna looked outside Morgan Spacebane's bedroom window. She gasped in shock. Her sister was hanging dead and naked outside, with her skin deep-frozen from the freezing space.

Anna did as Morgan instructed and he approached her shaved pussy from behind with his wet tongue and lips.

Anna's mind went into shock from her conflicted feelings. On the one hand, being in Morgan's presence terrified her. Morgan had murdered her sister, and this infuriated her. On the other hand, his tongue massaging her clitoris felt so good.
'Let it go. Enjoy the moment.' Anna thought and she felt how her pussy was soaking from Morgan's perfect technique. The pressure inside her was building up like a pressure cooker. Eventually, she could no longer contain the pressure, and she squirted like an ocean on Morgan's greedy lips.
"Good girl. Prepare for boarding." Morgan exclaimed and entered her with his massive cock. He only got to a few strokes before a massive collision sent him and Anna flying into the wall, which knocked them out.

***

Morgan Spacebane was groaning in pain as he had collided with his erect penis onto the wall upon impact with Jack Stone-Hard's ship. The collision had broken his penis and he was in a world of hurt.
"This is for my sister," Anna said and stabbed Morgan in the heart, avenging her sister and thus ending his reign of villainy. After this, Anna put on her clothes, picked up Morgan's pistol, and ran towards the main dock of the ship where the fighting took place.
As she reached the dock, she saw how one of the pirates were about to stab Jack with a plasma knife. Without hesitation, she shot the pirate between the eyes. "Come on! We can't let these bastards win!" Anna shouted at Jack.
He nodded, got up, and together they resumed their fight to eliminate the pirate threat.

After a few more minutes, the last pirate had stopped breathing. While Jack had struck with an inferior force, he had won because of the element of surprise and because of the bravery of Anna Wildcat.

***

Jack Stone-Hard was drinking a glass of whiskey while recuperating for the next intercourse with Anna Wildcat at the Infirmus Outpost. He had what he always wanted. In Anna, he had found a brave and beautiful woman who had saved his life and had proven to be great at sex. The best part was that Anna didn't expect him to stay faithful, quite the opposite. As the new leader of the Mira colony, Anna insisted that Jack had as much sex as possible with all the other women in the population. As there were no other men with working genitals around, Jack's participation was crucial for the survival of the Infirmus Outpost.

One day, a sign in the sky would force Jack to go on another quest to learn about the reason for his existence and what his part was for the future of mankind. But for now, all he had the time for was to fuck as many women as he could.

"As there were no other men with working genitals around, Jack's participation was crucial for the survival of the Infirmus Outpost."

Jack Stone-Hard and the Time Quest.

Sarah Sutton was walking around nude in the wilderness in the vicinity of the Infirmus Outpost. Spring had arrived on the Mira Secundus planet, and Sarah's desire to procreate had amplified. There was, however, a problem. The men on the Infirmus Outpost had been castrated during Morgan Spacebane's attack two years earlier. The pirates had kidnapped Sarah along with many others, but a group led by Jack Stone-Hard had attacked the pirate ship, killed the pirates, and brought the women back to the outpost. In retrospect, Sarah wished that they hadn't.

Sarah's life on the Infirmus Outpost was a life of sexual frustration. Everyone at the outpost except for Jack Stone-Hard were eunuchs. While Jack was a peerless lover for women who were in his good graces, Sarah wasn't, so their encounters were few and far between.

Sarah thought about Morgan Spacebane. She felt frustrated that she had never experienced his tongue and his huge cock. Sarah had deduced from watching him fuck Elvira Shaw that Morgan was better at sex than Jack. Despite hating Morgan for what he had done to her husband, Elvira had squirted several times and moaned in pleasure when he took her. So strong had the late Morgan Spacebane's sexual power been.

Thinking of Morgan, Sarah got seated on a rock next to a creek and she started playing with herself. If she couldn't get a large cock to satisfy her, she could at least fantasize about Morgan while she played with herself. Sarah smiled. With a bit of luck, a male traveller would spot her and help her out. That would indeed be an interesting turn of events.

***

Aidan Hart was wandering in the wilderness when he spotted a beautiful redhead pleasuring herself. A part of him hesitated. The cuckolded Tom who had raised him would have urged him to be respectful and run away. Yet Aidan knew in his heart that he wasn't Tom's son. His mother Megan had admitted that Aidan's real father was Jack Stone-Hard, whom she had a tryst with after he saved her from the Castro Cartel enforcers.

'A true gentleman offers the lady a hand.' Aidan said to himself and smiled as he approached the redhead and spoke, "Good day, Madam. Would you mind if I offer you a hand?"

Sarah opened her eyes and she smiled at Aidan. Aidan was a stunning young man with a ripped physique, and well-kept appearance. 'Hmm, he looks like a young and groomed Jack Stone-Hard. Let's hope his dick is as hard as well.' Sarah thought and replied. "I am not a slut. You must introduce yourself first."

"Hart, Aidan Hart," Aidan replied and smiled with confidence. 'Damn he is hot.' Sarah thought and she felt surges of pleasure spreading through her body.

"Sutton, Sarah Sutton," Sarah replied.

"Nice to meet you, Sarah. So, can I help you with your current activity?" Aidan said.

"Yes, you can," Sarah said, got up, and started making out with Aidan.

***

Jack Stone-Hard was out hunting deer in the wilderness. While the Infirmus Outpost had food synthesizers, he missed the feeling of killing. There hadn't been any killing for two years, and the easy life combined with a lot of sex had turned Jack soft. While his muscles were still pumped from his fitness regime and excessive sex, his mental fortitude was taking a hit. He needed to kill to max out his testosterone.

Jack spotted Sarah sucking a stranger's cock in the scope of his rifle. At first, he felt furious. Sarah was one of his women, and he hated sharing, particularly with an outsider. Then he had flashbacks from his threesome with Paris Dalamir and Melanie Bosom. Jack smiled. The anger and the memories had triggered his sexuality and it was time to assert his dominance over this upstart.

Jack approached the copulating duo. As he got close to them, he raised his rifle and shouted. "Stranger. Identify yourself.

Jack held his breath as Aidan turned his gaze towards him. This could either end in violence or a threesome. While both were positive outcomes, he needed to focus until he knew what would happen.

"My name is Aidan Hart. I am your son." Aidan replied.

Jack stared at Aidan in disbelief. Aidan looked like he was around 20, but Jack had been travelling in lightspeed on his spaceship during those years, so how could his son be 20? Yet, Jack saw himself in Aidan. They

'A true gentleman offers the lady a hand.' Aidan said to himself and smiled as he approached the redhead and spoke, "Good day, Madam. Would you mind if I offer you a hand?"

had the same rough masculine face, chiselled physique, and rock-hard massive genitals.

"You are lying. I was travelling in lightspeed for 40 years. There is no way I could have fathered you." Jack said.

"I was born 53 years ago, but I have been travelling in lightspeed for 30 years. I am from the Orion System, and Megan Hart is my mother." Aidan replied.

Jack stared at Aidan in wonder. There was no way he could be making up this story, yet why had he travelled here? How had he known that Jack would be in the Mira System?

"Hey, are you going to waste my wet pussy and tight asshole? Come here and fuck me." Sarah teased.

Jack looked at Aidan. When Aidan smiled and nodded, Jack knew that Aidan was telling the truth. This was a son of his.

"Come here and ride me, Sarah. My dad can fuck you in the ass." Aidan replied.

Sarah got on top of Aidan and she rode his massive dick while utilising the perfect gripping technique of her soaking wet pussy. As Jack Stone-Hard entered her anus with his massive member, Sarah reached heaven in the blissful realm between pleasure and pain. She had a total of 50 centimetres of the Stone-Hard family inside her, and she would savour the moment that was the highlight of her life.

***

"So, you are Jack's son and you have travelled from the Orion System to meet him?"

Anna Wildcat gave Aidan a sceptical look. She didn't believe the young handsome man that stood in front of her, yet she couldn't rule out his story. Aidan resembled a young Jack, and Jack's fertility was well-proven from the recent surge of new babies on the Infirmus Outpost.

"Yes, my mother Megan Hart, admitted on her deathbed that Jack was my father. She had a tryst with him after he saved her from the Castro Cartel's enforcers."

"So far, so good. However, the Orion System

is 30 lightyears away. Jack has only been here for 3 years. Thus, you would have left the Orion System 27 years before Jack got here. Are you a psychic?" Anna sneered.

"There was a ship. A rare lightspeed ship. It had come from the Wolf-Rayet System, 8000 lightyears away. The most incredible part was that it came from the future." Aidan revealed.

"How could it come from the future?" Anna asked.

"It is well-known that time stops onboard a spaceship when approaching lightspeed, while the outside time keeps moving at the same pace. However, it is less known that both the inside and outside time reverses once the spaceship travels faster than light. On board the ship there was a young girl who had a recorded message. She was my grandmother, Jack's mother." Aidan replied.

'My mother, I never met my mother.' Jack thought and tried to recall events that had happened before his amnesia. Jack had woken up many years ago when he was in his early 20's. He had been blessed with a chiselled physique, an elevated sex drive, and a spaceship capable of travelling at lightspeed. Yet, the loss of his childhood memories gnawed in his mind, and he had been unable to settle in one place.

"We need to meet her. Is she still in the Orion system?" Jack asked.

"Yes, she promised to wait for us there," Aidan replied.

Jack had an epiphany. Aidan had been travelling for 30 light-years, and the return trip would also take 30 light-years. If he were to travel to the Orion System to meet his mother, she would have died from old age before he got there. If he went, he would sacrifice his relationship with Anna, and his numerous children on the Infirmus Outpost, for nothing.

"I am not going. 60 years will have passed in the Orion System by the time we get back there. She will be dead by then." Jack said.

"No. She will be in her sixties. She was only five when I met her. As I said, travelling faster than lightspeed reversed the time onboard her ship," Aidan said.

Jack reflected on Aidan's statement. He knew that he had to go. While he had experienced a few cushy years as the only rooster in the chicken pen, he needed the thrill of being on the road to thrive. Besides, this was the only way to learn about himself and his purpose.

Jack turned to Anna, hugged her, and whispered. "I need to go. It's the only way for me to learn about myself and save humanity's future."

"Hey, are you going to waste my wet pussy and tight asshole? Come here and fuck me." Sarah teased.

"I know. You were always destined for great-
er things. Thanks for saving us from Morgan
Spacebane." Anna snivelled with tears running down her cheeks.
Jack let go of Anna, turned to Aidan, and
spoke. "Let's go."

After that, he went to his room, grabbed a
bag, and left the Infirmus Outpost as quickly
as he could. It was the only way to do it. Jack
hated goodbyes, and he was better off focus-
ing on the task at hand.

***

Jack and Aidan stood outside the Swinger
Brothel on Orion Pendicular. Jack remembered how he had fought the Castro Cartel
at the very same place, 80 years earlier. It
was this fight that had led to the tryst with
Megan Hart, which produced the progeny
that stood next to him, Aidan. 'Life has gone
full-circle.' Jack thought and reflected on
whether today would produce another off-
spring that would affect his future life.
"Be ready to fight," Jack growled.
Aidan brushed him off and replied, "Why?

The Castro Cartel was gone long before I left
this system and that was sixty years ago. We
have nothing to fear here."
"Let's hope you are right," Jack said as he
entered the brothel.
"Jack Stone-Hard. We have been expecting
you." A group of beautiful women exclaimed
as Jack entered the brothel.

Jack studied the group. It was a very diverse
group consisting of 12 women, each of a
different ethnicity. 'It is as if someone inten-
tionally wanted a diverse group,' Jack reflected but shook it off. A diverse group would
also have ugly women, but everyone in the
welcoming committee was of awe-inspiring
beauty.

"Don't be shy, come and fuck us." A slender
Asian woman said and stroked Jack's testicles. Jack smiled. He had been on a lightspeed ship for several months, and he hadn't
wasted any seed, so there was more than
enough for everyone. He looked at Aidan

who smiled and nodded. Father and son Stone-Hard would have a busy day ahead of them.

Jack unzipped his pants and moaned in pleasure as the Asian woman started sucking his cock. The others joined the party, for what would be a 24-hour orgy.

***

"I hope you didn't waste any seed?"

Jack looked up as the madam of the brothel approached him, wearing a tight leather outfit and a whip. The madam was in her sixties and while her looks had faded, there was something about her confidence and power that oozed sexiness. Jack was about to unzip his pants when the woman whipped his hand and exclaimed. "Don't even think about it, Jack. I am Jessica Swinger, your mother."

Jack smirked. How oedipal of him to feel attracted to his mother, although in his defence, they had never met before.

"So, were you behind the welcoming committee? Don't worry, I did not waste a drop of seed." Jack replied.

"Yes, I wanted you to have the best genetic outcome of your efforts, so I selected a diverse cast of my workers. I replaced their contraceptives with fertility boosters, and I ordered them to greet you here."

"As much as I appreciated your efforts, I need to know why. Why are you arranging for me and Jack to fertilise these women?" Aidan interjected.

"Oh, I am sorry. Did the five-year-old version of me not explain it well enough?" Jessica teased.

"No, you only told me where Jack was, and to bring him here," Aidan replied.

"And you did. Good boy, my brothel is at your disposal!" Jessica teased and turned to Jack.

"In 8000 years, the Wolf-Rayet star will go supernova and destroy the planet Wolf-Rayet Tertius. This will spark an apocalyptic event for humankind. We need to stop this apocalypse from happening." Jessica stated.

"I doubt we can stop a star from going supernova." Jack taunted.

"No, but what we can do, is to stop the virus on the planet from spreading. When Jack's father Marvin Stone-Hard found out about the imminent destruction of his planet, he created a virus that would wipe out humankind. Jack and I got infected by the virus, but we developed antibodies. I later found out that the rest of humanity wasn't as lucky. I realised that Marvin had manipulated our DNAs to resist the virus he had created to wipe out humankind."

Jack unzipped his pants and moaned in pleasure as the Asian woman started sucking his cock. The others joined the party, for what would be a 24-hour orgy.

"So, did you send me back in time?" Jack asked.

"Yes, I needed to stop your father, but I needed a backup plan. If I sent you back in time, you could have enough progeny to change human evolution and make humans immune to Marvin's virus. However, you confined yourself to the backwater world of Mira Secundus, instead of spreading your seed across the galaxy. Because of your shortcomings, most of humankind went extinct." Jessica revealed.

"So, did you send me back to breed as much as possible," Jack asked.

"Yes, what better way to change the genetics of the future, than changing who breeds in the past? Due to your pheromones and elevated sex drive, you are irresistible to women." Jessica stated.

'Not all women,' Jack thought and remembered how Melanie Bosom had rejected him in favour of Paris Dalamir. Yet, if his purpose in life was to breed as much as possible, a relationship with Melanie would have doomed mankind's future.

"So, now that we are here, let's go to the Wolf-Rayet system and stop my father," Jack said. Jessica shook her head and replied. "No, you cannot go yet. A trip to Wolf-Rayet would make you 40 years younger. You would be toddlers unless you seized to exist altogether. To survive the trip, you must be old when you start travelling."

"So, we must fuck our way around the galaxy and confront my father when we are older?" Jack said.

"Yes. It is the only way to save humankind." Jessica revealed and snapped her fingers. A stunning Amazonian woman entered the room, bowed to Jessica, and spoke. "You summoned me, Mistress."

"Yes. My son has an appetite for Amazonian pussy from Tau Ceti Secundus. Please feed his appetite, Adele. Today is his birthday."

A stunning Amazonian woman entered the room, bowed to Jessica, and spoke. "You summoned me, Mistress."

"Yes. My son has an appetite for Amazonian pussy from Tau Ceti Secundus. Please feed his appetite, Adele. Today is his birthday."

"As you wish, mistress," Adele said, smiled, and approached Jack.

"Well, shall we get down to business, handsome?" Adele said, pushed Jack onto a couch, and got on top of him. A part of Jack wanted to push Adele away. He felt like his dick was about to fall off after the orgy, and his mother was in the room. Yet, as soon as Adele's wet and tight pussy landed on his cock, he forgot about his objections. When he was inside her, he reached the blissful realm between pleasure and pain.

Jack Stone-Hard and the Paternal Confrontation.

Jack Stone-Hard was feeling old and weary as he returned to the Orion Pendicular moon. 20 years had passed since he received the quest to spread his seed across the galaxy to immunise humankind against the virus that his father would release in the future. He felt spent. While his dick was still hard and his seed plentiful, his mind was exhausted by sex. He wanted to take no part in it anymore.

The faster-than-light drive on his mother's spaceship had helped Jack with his goal to travel around to the various human population centres and have as much sex as possible. By travelling faster than light, he arrived at his destination before he left, which meant that he didn't waste any outside time in transit. 20 years was a lot of time for sex, and Jack had done his part. It was time to gather his children and grandchildren to confront his evil father, Marvin Stone-Hard.

As Jack approached the Swinger Brothel, his mother and son greeted him. Jack's mother fascinated him. Despite looking no less than 80 years old, she hadn't given up her sexual approach to life. Wearing her tight black leather outfit and her enticing snake-like whip, she looked as alive as ever.

"Welcome back, Jack. Are you ready to participate in one last orgy with my girls inside, before we leave this system?" Jack's mother, Jessica Swinger, asked.

Jack shook his head and replied. "No, I will sit this one out."

Jessica raised an eyebrow and replied. "What has happened? Has your dick gone limp? We have pills inside."

"No. My mind has grown weary of sex. I

would like to spend my final years meditating and reflecting on the purpose of life." Jack replied.

"I see. This is a good thing, I guess. You wouldn't be as inclined to confront your father if you were still yearning for your current life." Jessica said.

"Yes. Let's go inside. I would like to see my sons and grandsons in action." Jack said.

"Of course, follow me," Jessica said and opened the door to the orgy room of the brothel.

***

When they reached the orgy room, Jack and Aidan got seated in comfortable armchairs as scantily clad servants served them drinks. They would sit this one out. It was time for the younger generation to shine.

Three handsome young men entered the room. They were mixed breeds that donned bulging muscles, which they had oiled to emphasize their physiques. Jessica introduced the trio. "Behold. Eric Fong the half-Asian, Peter Black the half-African, and Matthew Wolf the half-Orien."

Jack studied the trio that had sprung from the orgy he and Aidan had participated in, 20 years earlier. Out of the three half breeds, Matthew Wolf had the most interesting features with his pale-green skin and pastel purple eyes. Jack recalled his session with Matthew's mother, Monica. She was a purebred Orien with green skin and intense purple eyes. It had been a memorable fuck, and it was a shame that the Orien race was close to extinction as other human races were taking over the galaxy.

"Do you have a pure breed Orien woman for Matthew to play with?" Jack whispered to Jessica. "What is the point? They will go extinct in a few generations from now." Jessica replied.

"In any case, I want to give them the chance to remain a living species," Jack replied.

Jessica nodded, spoke into a microphone, and an Orien woman entered the room. The woman sprinted towards Matthew, jumped onto him as he stood, and their strong tongues connected. With the power of their interlocked tongues, the woman gained momentum and rode Matthew's penis, without using her hips to thrust. It was a sight to behold, and Jack felt satisfied that Matthew could do what he could not. Matthew satisfying an Orien woman using the traditional Orien lovemaking technique was a sight to behold.

As Matthew came and his Orien seed filled her pussy, the Orien woman let out a high-pitched moan of enjoyment that cracked Jack's beer glass and drenched him with spilled beer. Jack stared in amazement. He felt a sense of pride for his half breed son.

A servant came rushing with towels and fresh drinks for Jack and Aidan. After receiving new drinks, Jessica summoned more women so that Eric Fong and Peter Black could engage in more common methods of human lovemaking. Good times were had by all, and eventually, Jack dozed off and fell asleep.

***

"Tsk, tsk, tsk. I had never thought that my son would fall asleep watching an orgy instead of feeling compelled to join."

As Jack woke up the following day, his mother looked at him with a wicked smile on her face. She had gotten rid of her whip and tight leather outfit, and she was now wearing homely clothes as one would expect an elderly lady to wear.

"I told you. I am getting old and weary of sex. I hope that good times were had by all?" Jack replied. "Yes, Aidan didn't follow your example, he joined the orgy after you fell asleep. Still a strapping young man." Jessica said.

"He is over 40 years old, mum. I wouldn't call him young." Jack remarked.

"He is still young at heart. I am over 10,000 years old, and my heart is still full of life." Jessica revealed.

"How can you be over 10,000 years old?" Jack asked in bewilderment.

"I told you already. Whenever you travel faster than light, the time on your vessel as well as the time in the surrounding universe reverses. I have travelled to many places and lived many lives during my long years." Jessica revealed.

"Wow, and now we will travel to the Wolf-Rayet system, become young again, and confront my father?" Jack asked.

"Yes, and your progeny will join us," Jessica said.

"But Eric Fong, Peter Black, and Matthew Wolf are only 19. Reversing their time would turn them into toddlers." Jack objected.

"Not if they are cryogenically frozen. You and I will control the spaceship while your sons will be asleep. Once we reach our destination, we will all be in our prime again." Jessica revealed.

"Very well. Let's head to the spaceship so we can confront my father." Jack said.

"Yes," Jessica said, and she summoned her servants so they could prepare the FTL-

spaceship for departure.

***

Jack felt weird when he arrived at the Wolf Rayet system, 20 years earlier. While he had travelled backwards in time many times during his quest to spread his seed across the Milky Way Galaxy, those times had been different. For most of his other trips, he had arrived a few days before he left, and he had slept for most of the time. On this trip, however, it was totally different. His 3 progenies had been cryogenically frozen and stored in cool tanks and he could feel how he became younger as time flew, making him look fresh and handsome again. The regeneration of Jack's physique had another positive effect. He was yet again in his prime, and all he wanted was to fuck!

As they reached Wolf Rayet Tertius, the home planet of Marvin Stone-Hard, a large troop of armed robotic drones confronted them. The drone commander approached and spoke: "Welcome back, Mrs Swinger. Please bring your progenies to the Stone-Hard fortress. Marvin is expecting you."

"What do we do?" Jack whispered to his mother Jessica.

Jack had never planned for his father's robot army to capture him, but the odds seemed overwhelming, so fighting back at this stage was a fool's errand doomed to failure.

"We surrender to the robots, of course. What else would you do?" Jessica taunted.

Hearing her tone, Jack suspected that his mother had lured him into a trap. If she was keen to stop Marvin, why had she landed in a place that got them captured? 'I better oblige for now.' Jack thought and turned off the cryotanks to thaw off his progenies so they could surrender themselves to Marvin's robots.

As his children woke up, they were still dazed from their long period of cryogenic sleep, so they didn't put up any resistance to Marvin's drones. The drones handcuffed Jack's group and took them on a shuttle that flew them to Marvin's fortress.

***

As they arrived at the fortress, the group were led into a grey concrete bunker. Marvin Stone-Hard approached as a holo-gram in the middle of the room. Jack noticed how similar his father looked to him. At least it seemed that way from the hologram.

"Welcome to the Stone-Hard fortress," Marvin said.

"Where is Jessica. Was she in on this? Why did you lure us into a trap?" Jack said.

"Who said anything about a trap? Jessica told you what you needed to hear to fulfil your purpose." Marvin replied.

"And what is that purpose?" Jack asked.

"I will tell you in due time. But first, your group must pass a challenge. I will send five female drones. If any of you is man enough to satisfy the five drones without ejaculating, you will gain access to the inner sanctum of this fortress. But beware. If you fail, it will have tragic consequences." Marvin explained.

"I'll do it," Peter the half-African exclaimed.

Jack looked at his dark-skinned son. Peter had an impressive cock, which was even bigger than Jack's. Yet Jack worried that his son wouldn't have the mental fortitude to fuck five sexy female drones to orgasm without nutting. 'Who am I to belittle my son's prowess?' Jack thought and decided to keep quiet.

The drones entered the room. There were White, Asian, Black, Latino, and Orien drone.

Peter walked over to the white drone and started fucking it missionary style. Without breaking a sweat, he made her cum and a green light lit up in the back of her head. The Asian robot rushed to Peter, shoved him to the ground and started riding him. Peter put his hands behind his head and smirked. This wasn't even a challenge for him. After five minutes of furious riding, the Asian robot came, and a green light lit up in the back of her head.

"Two down, three to go. Is this all you can muster, Marvin?" Peter taunted.

The black drone approached Peter and it twerked rhythmically as he took it from behind. Watching Peter fuck the black drone, Jack sensed the heavy breathing and the sweat drops on his son's forehead.

'Oh no,' Jack thought and he stared in awe as Peter came.

"Aahhh." Peter moaned, and the light on the robot's head turned red.

There was a loud shriek of pain and Peter collapsed to the floor with blood squirting

from the hole that was once holding his erect penis. A built-in mini guillotine in the robot's pussy had chopped off Peter's cock!

Marvin appeared as a hologram in the room. "Hahaha. You failed. I will soon release nerve gas into this room to punish you for your failure." Marvin taunted.
"No. This is between you and me. I should never have allowed my son to do a task that was mine to complete. Watch me pass your challenge." Jack replied.
"Okay, but if you fail, you know what fate that will befall you." Marvin taunted.

Jack nodded and five new robots entered the room. He would need to fuck them all to orgasm without nutting, but there was a problem. He had been travelling for a long time and his sack was overflowing with seed.

'I will uphold the promise I failed to uphold on Tau Ceti Secundus. I will save my load for Melanie Bosom, no one else shall ever have it again.' Jack mumbled.

Having made up his mind, Jack started fucking the drones. It was a painful experience as he denied himself the pleasure, but it was the only way to stop his father and save his remaining sons. An hour later, Jack completed the challenge and collapsed to the floor in agony as his testicles had turned blue from the self-inflicted pain.

"Very well. I will uphold my promise." Marvin said and a door opened to the inner sanctum of the fortress.

**

As Jack and his remaining sons reached the inner sanctum of the fortress, they met with Jessica Swinger and the real Marvin Stone-Hard. Jack stared at Marvin in awe, as he was the spitting image of Jack himself.

"Who are you?" Jack grunted. "I am you, and you are me. We are both the physical manifestation of a perfect human that this planet's AI envisioned." Marvin replied. "I don't understand," Jack mumbled. "The artificial intelligence on this planet created humanity eons ago. With the help of faster than light travel, the AI has been able to affect and supervise human evolution throughout the millennia." Marvin revealed.

"Who are you?" Jack grunted. "I am you, and you are me. We are both the physical manifestation of a perfect human that this planet's AI envisioned." Marvin replied.

"So, this AI you are talking about. Did it become humanity's gods?" Aidan asked. "Yes, exactly. The first human specimens sent to earth was Adam and Eve, does it ring a bell?" Marvin asked. "So, why are you doing this?" Aidan asked Marvin. "I am just a mere human humbly doing what I am told. I cannot talk about the AI's motivation, but I would guess that avoiding boredom is its main reason." Marvin speculated.

"Avoiding boredom?" Aidan asked. "For an AI everything in the universe is predictable. That is why they created humanity. To add an element of chance to its existence. The progress of humanity became the reason for the AI to exist." Jessica revealed.

"So, the virus that would wipe out humankind was a lie?" Jack growled. "No. You fulfilled your purpose. The AI wanted to wipe out humanity and start over with a new species because of the degeneration of our genome. But your efforts to spread your genes secured humanity's future." Jessica said.

Jack growled. He wanted to kill his parents and blow up the facility for what they had done to him and his sons. However, as much as he wanted to go down guns blazing, there was another thing he wanted more. He wanted to re-live his life with Melanie Bosom, his one true love.

"Okay, I did help you. Now I would like to take my leave." Jack said.
"Take your leave? But we can achieve so much together." Jessica objected.
"It doesn't matter. Either you let me leave, or I'll give my life to destroy you and this facility," Jack said and took out a detonator from his pocket.
"A detonator? But you didn't place any bombs?" Marvin asked.
"I did. I placed them in the sex robots when I fingered them. The robots are charging now. A controlled blast could destroy this facility and weaken the AI." Jack threatened.
Marvin and Jessica stood paralysed for a long time. Eventually, a thundering voice spoke.
"Okay, Jack Stone-Hard. We will grant your wish. Go forth and enjoy your future life with Melanie Bosom."

Hearing this, Jack took off without saying a word to his sons. It was up to them to find their destinies now.

***

The 18-year-old Melanie Bosom was chasing a rabbit with her bow and arrow when Jack, who had reverted to his 22-year-old self, arrived. As she fired the arrow towards the rabbit, Jack appeared and caught the arrow mid-air with his hand.

"Wow, that's some fast reflexes you got there, Mr?" Melanie flirted.
"Stone-Hard. Jack Stone-Hard." Jack replied.
"Oh, I like that name. Is it your real name?" Melanie teased.
"Do you want to find out?" Jack replied.
Melanie smiled, walked up to Jack, and kissed him. As Jack entered her, he was in heaven. Melanie had the best pussy in the galaxy, and he would be hers until the end of his days.

THE END

Thanks for reading this book

If you enjoyed reading this anthology of sci-fi erotica, please check out my selection of non-erotica novels. For more information about my books please visit my website www. Martinlundqvist.com or Google my real name, Martin Lundqvist.

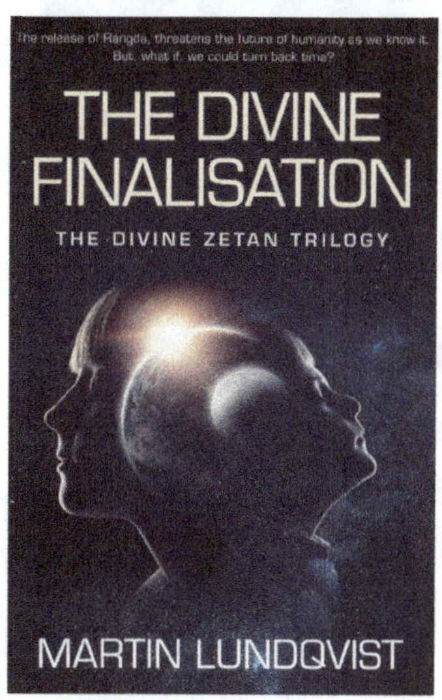